TELLING TALES
14 STORIES TO SHARE WITH YOUNG CHILDREN

by
Faye Stanley & Stuart Stotts

BIG VALLEY PRESS

Summary: Fourteen folktales to tell young children, with additional storytelling information.

We are primed to use stories.

Part of our survival as a species depended

upon listening to the stories of our tribal elders

as they shared parables and passed down

their experience and the wisdom

of those who went before.

-Philippa Perry

Table of Contents

INTRODUCTION

**Listening children know stories are there.
When their elders sit and begin, children are just
waiting and hoping for one to come out,
like a mouse from its hole.**
– Eudora Welty

We've told stories to children and families for many years, and we're still amazed at the power of a folktale to focus attention, to draw in an audience, and to stimulate the imaginations of old and young. Storytelling is one of the oldest art forms, rooted in the evolutionary processes of the human brain.

Storytelling is a fantastic tool for teachers and parents, a craft that does not require a huge investment of time and energy. We probably can't teach you to play the guitar or weld a metal sculpture in a few hours, but you can learn to tell simple stories with only limited instruction or study, and a little bit of practice. We hope that this text will provide the resources needed for you to begin that journey.

In our experience, the two most common obstacles to becoming an active storyteller are courage and repertoire. It takes courage to close the book and rely on one's own memory, skills, and imagination, particularly in the beginning. But our own history with teaching folks to tell stories has convinced us that once a teller takes the leap, they are rewarded with the enthusiasm and engagement of their listeners. They also often experience many unexpected, joyful interactions, deepening the relationships of all involved. It is the magic of shared story.

Repertoire is the second challenge. You will have to invest time, practice, and a bit of your soul to tell a story. Remember to choose and develop stories for telling that you like and enjoy. With a multitude of stories from which to choose (not to mention those you make up!), there's no need to squander your storytelling energies on something with which you don't feel a real connection. However, finding that perfect story and building your repertoire is probably the biggest challenge for the beginning storyteller. It can take a lot of work to research stories, read through collections, and be able to recognize a story that will work for you and your audience. The aim of this book is to make that task simpler and less time consuming for you, the busy teacher or parent of young children.

There are literally thousands of folktale collections. It's important to find stories that are appropriate for children between the ages of 3 and 6, as many tales are too scary, violent, long, or complicated. While an experienced storyteller might be able to adapt and perform a greater range of stories for young children, beginning tellers need stories that are short, clear, and developmentally appropriate for little ones.

This book is intended to help with the challenge of repertoire. We've chosen stories that are relatively short, are appropriate for young children, and that beginning storytellers can learn and present quickly. You will most assuredly find that some of these tales appeal to you, while others do not. The choices you make represent the first steps in finding your own storyteller's voice.

We believe that young children should hear folktales. It's also important that they hear contemporary stories, and experience picture books, and make up their own stories. But folktales touch a deep source of humanity. They've survived for generations because they carry some truth that bears repeating. They can also carry a sense of a culture, a people, place, and time that is different from our own, providing a window into the broader, lived experiences of others. They can serve to bring us together by highlighting our shared humanity.

In general, you'll find that this collection steers away from stories that include morals or draw the point of the story into a summarizing sentence. The interaction of the listener with the story provides an important opportunity for a young child to create meaning and synthesize the events of the story into their own lived experience. Folktales are a rich canvas onto which listeners, including young children, can project and build their own understandings.

In this book you will find stories that include the important considerations for telling to young children—stories that are short and stories that have repetition. Either or both of these factors are very helpful for the beginning storyteller. Short stories are easy to remember, and stories with repetition allow students to anticipate the action, and for you to build in opportunities for their participation. You may want to pause and teach repeated parts to children, adding gestures or movements, to make sure they can participate successfully with you. You may find that these repetitive moments in the telling will become the most enthusiastically received portions of the tale.

We don't feel the need to use puppets, flannel boards, or illustrations in storytelling. There's nothing wrong with this approach at times, although it may distract from the imagery produced in the child's own imagination. There may be times, however, when children need background knowledge prior to hearing the stories. They may need to see a picture of a koala, for example, or talk about how plants grow, in order to understand the stories better.

We encourage you to watch other storytellers. To that end, we've included a short list of storytelling websites in the resource section. Remember too, that any opportunity at a library, school assembly, or storytelling festival that allows you to observe storytellers in action will model "how it's done," and bolster your learning process.

The real first rule of storytelling is to have fun doing it. (This is, again, why it is so important to choose stories for telling that you like!) Your joy in the telling is at the heart of what makes for success. Take pleasure in your own tale-telling, and bask in the delight on the faces of the children. We think you'll become a convert to the power of storytelling.

Faye Stanley and Stuart Stotts

Chapel Hill, North Carolina and Deforest, Wisconsin
2015

Acknowledgements

We are grateful to a wide community of storyteller and educators who have worked with us in a variety of settings over the last thirty years.

In particular, the teaching artists and staff who are part of the Kennedy Center Education Department have provided us with support, inspiration, and deep learning about the arts and their role in curriculum, culture, and classroom. It has been a place where we have had the opportunity to connect with others committed to arts integrated education, and where we met each other as well. We offer particular gratitude to Amy Duma and Lynne Silverstein.

Storytellers as a whole are a generous bunch, and we've learned a great deal from formal or informal interactions with many tellers. We'd like to offer special thanks to Joe Hayes, Bill Harley, Jim May, Kevin Kling, Jackie Torrence, Sid Lieberman, Susan Gilchrist, Elizabeth Matson, Bill Harley, and Jon Spellman.

We also thank our families and friends, and the many teachers and children who have nourished our stories with their energy and enthusiasm. How fortunate to live a life filled with shared stories!

THE NUTS AND BOLTS
OF STORYTELLING

"Stories have to be told or they die, and when they die, we can't remember who we are or why we're here."
-Sue Monk Kidd

There are many things that tellers do to make a story interesting, engaging, or participatory. While this book provides choices in beginning repertoire for parents and early childhood teachers, this section offers a short introduction to the basic tools storytellers use to tell stories. Whole books have been written about these tools, and if you want to explore them in greater depth, you can find further support and ideas in the Resources section of this book. Additionally, we offer online courses to support the acquisition and skills of storytelling, and those are listed in the Resource section as well.

As you explore these tools, think about how you might utilize them in your own telling. Notice how your choices in using them serve to effectively reflect the quality of a character, the emotion of an event, or the type of experience you want your listeners to have as you share the story.

Voice

One of the most important tools you have as a teller is your voice. Consider these possibilities in the use of your voice as a storytelling tool:

VOICE ELEMENTS FROM YOUR STORYTELLER'S TOOLBOX

Intensity • Mood • Attitude

- detached
- obsessive
- playful
- driven
- light

- matter-of-fact
- somber
- depressed
- playful
- anxious

- careless
- joyful
- submissive
- dejected
- arrogant

- desperate
- sly
- domineering
- sullen
- frightened

Pacing • Speed • Pauses

- frantic
- relaxed
- calm

- quick
- slow & lazy
- moderate
- plodding

- for movement
- for sound effects
- for sign language
- for dramatic effect

Pitch • Accents • Tone Quality

- high
- mid-range
- low
- breathy

- regional
- language-based
- national
- squeaky

- gravelly
- smooth

Sound Effects

- growl
- roar
- pant
- laugh

- shriek
- snarl

- howl
- animal sounds
- mouth sounds

Volume

- whispered
- very soft
- soft
- medium level
- loud
- very loud

Gesture/Body

Similarly, consider how much you communicate about characters, or even about how you are feeling about telling the story, through your body. Consider the following aspects of body language as tools in your storytelling practice:

BODY LANGUAGE ELEMENTS FROM YOUR STORYTELLER'S TOOLBOX

Eyes • Face			
• frightened	• shifty	• open	• animated
• wide	• questioning	• wizened	• calculating
• relaxed	• hooded	• compressed	• sneering
• sleepy	• direct	• loose	• enraged
• narrowed	• kind	• prune-faced	

Attitude			
• haughty	• confident	• playful	• needy
• nurturing	• joyful	• curious	• deceptive
• teasing	• tense	• expectant	• fearful
• hopeful	• strong	• lost	• alluring
• trusting	• agitated	• anxious	
• disoriented	• uncaring	• worried	

Finally, think about the intentional movements you might incorporate into your telling of the story.

Gestures

This may include any gestures that are rhythmically produced (based on a steady beat) as well as those that are done in connection with a particular word or moment in the story. These are often sequences of gestures, or gestures that accompany song or chant.

- gestures that indicate movement such as rolling, falling, flying, etc.
- gestures that indicate direction or describe in some way
- gestures that are more abstract, included for rhythmic, or other interest

---

Sign Language

Don't forget the fabulous opportunities for including sign language in your tellings. This is developmentally especially useful with young children, and you'll find they respond with great enthusiasm to the inclusion of these types of symbolic gestures.

Find signs for specific characters, objects, or actions at
ASLPro.com

LEARNING A STORY

Of course, the reality is that in order to tell a story, you must learn a story. There are ways to do that that will make it easier and faster to learn a tale for telling. Be aware that these techniques can be particularly useful if you are afraid of forgetting the sequence of the story. Learned this way, you'll find learning stories a simple process, and one that gets easier with each story you undertake to learn.

There is, of course, no substitute for practice in learning a story for telling. For example, if you teach in a school with a couple of other classrooms, trade time with coworkers and tell your story to their classes as well. After the third time, you'll have a pretty good sense of the sequence, flow, pacing, and techniques involved. After the tenth time, the story is yours forever. Fortunately for us as storytellers, willing young children are happy to accommodate our need for repetition, often requesting that the same story be told over and over again.

The addition of one or two stories to your repertoire that you tell rather than read every year will have you becoming an accomplished and proficient teller more quickly than you could possibly imagine.

The method here is easy, quick, and effective. The repetitions called for may be executed in front of a mirror, a wall, to the dog, in the shower. One of my favorite spots for this is while driving or walking. Remember, don't be critical of yourself, just muddle through from beginning to end!

Quick and Easy Method for Learning a Story

1. Read the story through twice, out loud.

2. Determine the story elements, the "story's bones": setting, characters, sequence of events (incidents), conflict, crisis, resolution.

3. Draw the story in boxes, with each major event in a box of its own (like a comic strip). Set them up sequentially, so every story event is notated. Don't worry about your drawing skills—even stick figures are fine for this purpose, or symbols that represent your characters.

4. Try telling the story in your own words using only your comic strip for guidance. Use natural language; do not try to memorize the story word for word. Just muddle through the tale, visualizing in sequence what happened, when, where, and why. Do this twice.

5. Try telling the story using any sound effects, characterizations, facial expressions, and gestures that you have developed. Again, don't try to memorize, just muddle your way through. Do this twice.

6. Go back and isolate your first and last sentences. Actually memorize these two sentences, always telling them exactly the same way. This will give you confidence, and provide the well-thought-out ending with the punch needed to wrap up the story effectively.

7. Practice the story with your memorized beginning and ending, your voice, body and rhythm elements, and your own words throughout.

8. Tell it! If at all possible, tell the story multiple times within a few days. You will find that the immediate feedback provided by your listeners gives you ideas for changes. Make the changes as they come up for you. This process goes on for a long time, and you will be surprised how easily and naturally these changes will come into your telling. Have fun!

THE
STORIES

Sweet Porridge

This story is adapted from Grimm's Fairy Tales. In the mid 1800s Jacob and Wilhelm Grimm gathered folktales in Germany and published various collections of them. Their work has provided a foundation of repertoire for storytellers and writers around their world. While many stories from this famous collection are not suitable for young children, Sweet Porridge is a timeless favorite. SS

There was once a little girl who lived alone with her mother. They were very poor and had little to eat.

One day the girl went walking in the forest, carrying only a crust of bread and some water. Deep in the woods she met an old woman. The girl greeted her kindly and offered to share her bread and water. The old woman gladly accepted.

After they had eaten together, the old woman offered the girl a magic pot.

"You don't ever need to be hungry again," said the woman. "If you say,

'Cook, little pot, porridge sweet.
Cook little pot, so we can eat'

it will make good sweet porridge. Say,

'Stop little pot, no more stuff.
Stop, little pot, we've had enough'

and it will stop.

The child thanked the old woman and brought the pot home to her mother, and they no longer had to worry about food. When they were hungry, the little girl said,

"Cook, little pot, porridge sweet.
Cook little pot, so we can eat"

and the pot was filled with good sweet porridge. When they had eaten enough, the girl said,

"Stop little pot, no more stuff.
Stop, little pot, we've had enough"

and the pot was empty again.

One day, when the girl was out, the mother said,

"Cook, little pot, porridge sweet.
Cook little pot, so we can eat."

The pot cooked, and she ate her fill, but when she wanted the pot to stop, it wouldn't, because she had forgotten the magic words. She tried saying, "Stop pot" and "Quit cooking," and "That's enough," but nothing worked.

The pot went right on cooking, and filled up the pot until it overflowed. It kept on cooking. Soon the kitchen and the whole house were full. Then the house next door and the whole street were overflowing with porridge.

No one knew what to do. People were covered in porridge as it poured down the streets like a muddy river.

When there was only one single house left unfilled, the girl came back. She saw what was happening and said,

"Stop little pot, no more stuff.
Stop, little pot, we've had enough."

The pot stopped and was empty again. But anyone who wanted to get back to town had to eat their way through all the sweet porridge.❖

Notes on Telling:

Children will probably need to know what porridge is. Oatmeal is the best explanation. You might want to tell this story after making or serving oatmeal. The girl and the old woman characters present a good opportunity to employ different voices. Children can learn the magical chant, and tellers may want to expand the story in order to repeat the chant a couple more times. The chant can be accompanied by a magical gesture, and children can also add motions for eating and stirring. SS

A Drop of Honey

A tale from Burma and Thailand This wonderful story has the feel of a train wreck you can see coming for miles. It also has, as do many folktales, an important bit of wisdom for all of us. When we expect to pass along troublesome issues to others rather than actively commiting ourselves to their resolution, there can be disastrous consequences for us as individuals, as well as for our communities. FS

Once there was a king, hanging out on his balcony high above the town. He was eating sweet cakes with the queen, and they were laughing and talking. As the king laughed, a drop of sweet honey dripped from his delicious pastry onto the balcony rail. His wife said, "My dear, you have dripped honey on the rail. Let's call someone to clean it up!" She was about to do that, when the King said,

Honey that spills is just not worth my time.
I assign that to my minion.
Tiny details are just not our concern, you should
Delegate, in my opinion.

So, the two of them continued eating, and talking and laughing. The sun shone, and the honey grew warm, and slowly dripped from the rail down onto the street below.

The Queen noticed this, and said, "My dear, that honey has dripped down onto the street, and it's attracting flies. Let's call someone to clean it up!" But again the King responded:

Honey that drips is just not worth my time.
I assign that to my minion.
Tiny details are just not our concern, you should
Delegate, in my opinion.

Then a lizard came, and with his quick tongue began to catch the flies. And then a cat came, and began to bat that lizard around, and then a dog came and began to nip at the cat.

The Queen, looking down on the ruckus below, said, "Husband! Those flies have attracted a lizard, who attracted a cat, who is being attacked by a dog! Shouldn't we call someone to stop the fight?"

An animal fight is just not worth my time.
I assign that to my minion.
Tiny details are just not our concern, you should
Delegate, in my opinion.

Well, the baker down below saw the dog biting her cat, and ran out and started hitting the dog with a rolling pin. The butcher saw the baker hitting his dog, and came out and started swiping at the cat with a broom. Before long the butcher and baker were swatting each other! When the neighbors heard all the racket, they went outside and got into it, too. Then some soldiers came by, and since they all knew the butcher and baker, they started taking sides and got into the fight, too. Before long, it was a huge battle in the streets. People were throwing rocks through windows, knocking over things, and then someone threw a torch through a window. A fire started, and quickly spread to the palace itself. The King and Queen were escorted out of the palace and rushed out into the countryside, away from the fire.

Later that day, when the fire had at last been put out, the King and Queen were walking through the ruins of their town. The King stopped, leaned over and dipped his finger in a small puddle. "Ah, honey!" he said.

A small drop of honey may just be worth my time,
For that, we've lost the whole kingdom.
Tiny details are everyone's concern –
Details, and how we all fix 'em. ❖

Notes on Telling:

I have inserted a chant into this tale that may provide for some fun, repeated gestures. Try inventing those movements with your students. Don't always feel that the movements you create need to "act out" the words. Rhythmic movements such as claps, snaps, stamps, etc., may have no meaning, but provide just the playful emphasis this story needs. FS

The Turnip

This story is also adapted from the Grimm Fairy Tales. Joanne Oppenheim wrote a sweet picture book called "One Gift Deserves Another," based on the original Grimm tale. SS

Once upon a time there were two brothers. One, named Will, became rich, though he was a lazy and sometimes mean man. The other, named Jack, worked hard but never seemed to have any money. Although they lived in the same village, they rarely even saw each other.

Will lived in a big house and did little all day.

Jack lived in a small shack outside of town. He decided to grow a garden, and he planted turnips. He put the seeds in the ground, covered them up, watered them, and waited for them to sprout.

A few days later, the seeds poked their heads through the soil. Jack cared for them, and they began to grow.

But one turnip grew much larger than the rest. One week it was as big as an orange. The next, it was a big as a watermelon. The next, as big as a donkey. The next as big as a wagon, and the next, as big as Jack's house.

What should he do with the turnip? Jack thought and thought, and then he decided to give it to the king. He borrowed a huge wagon and four oxen, and with his neighbors' help, he loaded the turnip onto the wagon.

The king was very surprised at this unusual gift. "One gift surely deserves another," said the king. "How should I reward you?" He paused, and then called to his servant. "We must reward this man. Bring gold and silver and fine clothing."

Jack's wagon was loaded with this wealth, and he returned to his house. He built himself a fine house, and continued to grow his garden.

One day Will came walking in Jack's neighborhood. He saw Jack's giant house, and he understood that Jack was rich. Will was jealous. He knocked on Jack's door.

Jack welcomed his brother in. Will looked around at the beautiful furniture. He asked Jack how he came to be so rich. Jack told him that he had given the king a magnificent turnip and had been rewarded with gold, silver, and fine clothes.

Will went home and thought to himself, "If the king gave Jack so much for just a turnip, how much more would he give me if my gifts were even more valuable?" He loaded up his wagon with his own gold, silver, and fine clothes and headed to the palace.

The king looked at the many gifts that Will had brought. He looked carefully at Will. "One gift surely deserves another," said the king. "How shall I reward you?"

He thought a while, and then called to his servant. "We must reward this man with something special." He paused, and then ordered, "Bring the turnip."

Will returned to his house with the giant turnip on his wagon. He was a poorer but wiser man. And all through the winter, at least he had enough to eat. ❖

Notes on Telling:

Children might not know what a turnip is. You can either show them one, or you can substitute another garden plant: watermelon, tomato, potato, etc. You can add gestures to demonstrate the size of the turnip, the difficulty of pulling and carrying it, and the work of planting. You can also use facial expressions to show the characters' reactions to the turnip and the gifts from the king. And it's fun to let the king speak in a kingly manner. SS

The Little Red Hen

This familiar, traditional North American tale has many versions, and, of course, an important message for all of us. As is true of many folktales, this important message is provided with glorious playfulness rather than finger-wagging admonishment. FS

One day the Little Red Hen was out pecking in the farmyard, and she came upon some wheat kernels. Well, Little Red Hen had an idea. "If I plant them, we will have wheat, and can make bread to eat.... Yum!"

So, she called out to her friends in the farmyard: "Who will help me plant this wheat?"

"Not I," said the cat, as she scratched at her ear, "for me it is much too hard."

"Not I," said the dog, as he chewed his bone, "it is time that I dig in the yard."

"Not I," said the pig, as he rolled on his back, "the mud is where I want to be."

"I guess that means," said the Little Red Hen, "that it all comes down to me."

The Little Red Hen prepared the soil for the kernels of wheat. She planted them, and took care of them every single day. At long last, the kernels had grown into tall stalks of wheat.

"Who will help me cut this wheat?" called the Little Red Hen.

"Not I," said the cat, as she scratched at her ear, "for me it is much too hard."

"Not I," said the dog, as he chewed his bone, "it is time that I dig in the yard."

"Not I," said the pig, as he rolled on his back, "the mud is where I want to be."

"I guess that means," said the Little Red Hen, "that it all comes down to me."

And that's just what she did. She cut down the wheat and threshed it 'til she had a big sack of grain.

"The grain is ready to be taken to the miller, and ground into flour," said the Little Red Hen. "Who will help me carry it to the mill?"

"Not I," said the cat, as she scratched at her ear, "for me it is much too hard."

"Not I," said the dog, as he chewed his bone, "it is time that I dig in the yard."

"Not I," said the pig, as he rolled on his back, "the mud is where I want to be."

"I guess that means," said the Little Red Hen, "that it all comes down to me."

So that's just what she did. She hoisted the big, heavy sack of grain on her back, and carried it, all by herself, all the way to the miller. The miller ground that wheat into nice light flour, and the Little Red Hen carried it all the way home.

"The flour is ready to be made into a cake," said the Little Red Hen. "Who will help me cook?"

"Not I," said the cat, as she scratched at her ear, "for me it is much too hard."

"Not I," said the dog, as he chewed his bone, "it is time that I dig in the yard."

"Not I," said the pig, as he rolled on his back, "the mud is where I want to be."

"I guess that means," said the Little Red Hen, "that it all comes down to me."

And that's just what she did. She went to work with her fresh flour, adding butter and sugar and milk and salt and raisins. Little Red Hen missed everything together in a big bowl, and then put it all in the oven.

Soon a wonderful smell filled the kitchen, drifting out across the farmyard. The Little Red Hen took her cake out of the oven, and said, "Now it is time to eat. Who will help me eat?

"I will!" said the cat, leaping down from her perch, "I'm happy to help where I can!"

I will!" said the dog, as he ran that way, "You can serve mine up in a pan!"

"I will," said the pig, and he rolled over quick, stood up, and gave the mud a shake.

"Oh no, you won't," said the Little Red Hen, "I alone will eat this cake!

You didn't help me plant, or harvest or carry, or bake or do any work at all.

So now the work is over, and it's time to eat, don't be running over here when I call!" ❖

Notes on Telling:

The chant created for this version of the story has great potential to be shared among individuals or small groups, after you have told it a few times. Allow students to create gestures or movements to accompany their portion of the chant. Their creative contributions to the telling will only enhance the fun! I particularly like to wag my finger on the repeated line, "And that's just what she did!" I find students love doing this! FS

The Three Wishes

Another Grimm story. The original tale has a wood sprite in the tree, but a teacher in a workshop suggested changing that to a magic squirrel, to make the idea more immediate. The change stuck in my telling. So many of the Grimm stories are about food, which must reflect the hardships and hunger common in everyday people's lives. SS

Once upon a time a poor woodcutter went to the woods to chop a tree. He came to a part of the forest where he had never been. He spotted a large and beautiful tree. As he raised his axe, he heard a voice from the tree cry out.

"Please don't cut down this tree. It's my home."

It was a squirrel that spoke, sitting high on a branch.

"Very well," said the woodcutter.

"Since you are so kind, I will give you three wishes," said the squirrel.

The woodcutter headed home. He didn't believe in magic. When he got home, he sat at the table. His wife served him a crust of bread and bowl of thin soup for supper.

"Is this all there is? I wish I had a big sausage," he said.

Suddenly a fat juicy sausage appeared on his plate.

"Where did that come from?"' asked his wife.

The woodcutter remembered the squirrel's words. He explained what had happened to him. Immediately, his wife began to complain and insult the woodcutter. "How could you waste a precious wish on something as small as a sausage? We could have had a fine home, or good clothes, or gold, but, no, instead, you waste a magical wish on a sausage."

"Woman, quiet. Enough. You always attack me." They argued back and forth, their voices rising, until the woodcutter burst out with, "I wish this sausage were on your nose."

Instantly, the sausage was attached to her face.

"What have you done? Take it off right now," she yelled.

"If I do, I don't ever want to hear that I wasted a wish."

"Yes, yes. Just take it off."

The woodcutter made his final wish, to remove the sausage. He and his wife lived the rest of their days as poor as they ever were. But at least they had a sausage to eat that night. ❖

Notes on Telling:

Children may need to hear something about woodcutting as a profession. It's very common in folktales, and yet has little meaning today. The voices of the squirrel, the man, and the woman can help distinguish characters, but be careful when the man and woman are arguing that the voice for one doesn't inadvertently slip into the voice of the other. Gestures for the sausage on the nose can provoke laughter, and dramatic facial expressions throughout the story will draw children into the narrative. SS

Stone Soup

This story is a perennial favorite. There are hundreds of versions in books, recordings, videos, and music. I first heard this story from my father, his vivid account shared with me while traveling in the car. Its origin is in dispute, but in some cultures buttons, nails, and even an axe replace the stones. SS

Once there were two travellers who arrived at a village. They were tired and hungry, but when they knocked on people's doors and asked for something to eat, either no one answered, or they were rudely told to leave.

They didn't know it at the time, but soldiers had recently attacked the village and taken most of the villagers' food. The villagers just wanted to be left alone.

When the two travellers realized that no one would help them, they stood in the middle of the village and loudly said, "I guess we'll have to make some stone soup. And when it's done, we'll share it with everyone." They looked at each other and sang a song.

Stone soup, Stone soup.
Cooking up a pot of good stone soup.

Behind their doors, the villagers whispered to each other. "Who ever heard of stone soup?" And they peeked out to see what would happen.

The travellers gathered up some wood and made a fire. They pulled a large iron pot out of their backpack, filled it with water, and hung it over the flames. Then they looked on the ground and found three stones, each about the size of a fist. They rinsed off the stones and lowered them into the water.

"This stone soup will be so delicious," one of them said loudly, and they both began to sing and stir.

Stone soup, Stone soup.
Cooking up a pot of good stone soup.

A few curious villagers peered out of their windows to watch.

The water finally boiled. After it had simmered for some time, one of the travellers took a spoon from his bag and tasted the soup.

"Oh, this is delicious," he said. "Simply delicious. But it would taste better with some onions."

One of the villagers who was listening opened up his door. "I have some onions."

"Well, by all means, bring some here," said one of the travellers.

When the villager brought out the onions, they cut them up and added them to the soup. The villager stayed to watch, and joined the travellers as they sang and stirred.

Stone soup, Stone soup.
Cooking up a pot of good stone soup.

After a while, one of the travellers tasted the soup again.

"Ah, delicious. If only there were some carrots, though."

Another villager who was listening at his window called out, "I have some carrots."

"Bring them, if you like, and share our soup when it's done."

The carrots were added to the soup. The villager sat down to watch. They joined in singing, a little louder this time, as the travellers stirred.

Stone soup, Stone soup.
Cooking up a pot of good stone soup.

In similar fashion, one villager at a time brought potatoes, garlic, peppers, beans, and even cheese. Each of them stayed to watch the soup boiling, each of them helped to stir, and each of them joined in singing.

Stone soup, Stone soup.
Cooking up a pot of good stone soup.

When everything had cooked long enough, the villagers brought bowls and spoons, and the travellers ladled out enough soup for each person. It was delicious. After they had eaten, they sang again.

Stone soup, Stone soup.
Cooking up a pot of good stone soup.

When the travellers departed the next morning, they left the stones behind, in case the villagers ever wanted to make soup again.

They also left the song, which the villagers sang every time they made the recipe.

Stone soup, Stone soup.
Cooking up a pot of good stone soup. ❖

Notes on Telling:

You can use the song as a chant or improvise a melody. Children can suggest vegetables to add to the soup, and they can mimic motions of stirring, chopping, and tasting. You can add as many vegetables as you like. You might want to actually cook a version of stone soup with children bringing vegetables to add to the feast. SS

Grandmother Spider
Steals the Sun

A version of this story can be found in "American Indian Myths & Legends" by Richard Erdoes and Alfonso Ortiz. It was reportedly collected by James Mooney in the 1890s. SS

Once upon a time, animals and people lived together. It was a part of the world where there was only darkness. Nobody could see anything. Everyone kept bumping into one another, bonking their heads and tripping on each other's feet.

"We need light," one of the animals said, and all of the others agreed. But where would they find light?

Fox thought a long time and then he said, "I've heard that there are some people on the other side of the earth with lots of light, but they don't want to share it. They're too greedy and want to keep it all for themselves. Maybe we could get some their light?"

"How will we get this light?" asked the animals. "You said they don't want to share."

"Someone could steal it," said Fox.

Possum was the first to volunteer. He said he'd go steal some light. "I'll hide the light inside my bushy tail. They won't notice me as I run away."

Possum headed out for the other side of the earth. The sun was hanging in a tree, lighting everything up. It was so bright he could barely look at it.

Possum sneaked over and picked a little piece of sun from the tree and hid it in his tail. But that sun was so hot it burned all of the fur off of his tail. The people caught Possum and took the light back. They let Possum go, and he returned without the sun. But ever since then, Possum has a bald tail, not a bushy one.

"I'll try, " said Buzzard. "I won't put the light in my tail. I'll hide it in the feathers on my head."

But the same thing happened. When Buzzard tried to hide the sun in his head feathers, the sun burned them all away. The people caught Buzzard, took back the sun, and sent Buzzard away. He returned home without the sun, but ever since then, Buzzard has had a bald head.

The animals were going to give up, but Grandmother Spider said, "Let me try." She was so small they didn't think she could do it, but they agreed to give her a chance.

Grandmother Spider took some clay and made a thick round pot out of it. Then she spun a web that reached all the way to the other side of the earth. She was so small that none of the people noticed her as she crawled toward the light.

Grandmother Spider grabbed some light from the tree, put it in her clay bowl and hurried back home. The heat from the sun baked the clay solid, making a pot that could hold water or food or oil.

Now there was light for everyone. The animals celebrated and had a giant feast with music, dancing, and stories. Grandmother Spider not only brought the sun to the Cherokee people, she also taught them the art of making and baking pottery. ❖

Notes on Telling:

It's good to acquaint children with the animals in the story. In particular, Possum and Buzzard may be unfamiliar to them. You can use facial expression and gestures as you mime approaching and hiding the sun. This story might go well when you are making things from clay or play dough, and children might enjoy seeing examples of Cherokee or other Native American pottery. SS

The Lion and the Mouse

This is a classic Aesop story. Children love this tale because they are so aware of size and power differentials in their lives. You can find many versions of the story, from Aesop collections to picture books. SS

Once upon a time a Lion was asleep in the afternoon sun in the jungle. A little Mouse began running up and down on him, scurrying from his tale to his great mane.

The Lion woke up and trapped the Mouse with his huge paw. The Mouse squirmed and wiggled but couldn't get free. The Lion opened his big jaws to swallow him.

"I'm sorry, Great King," cried the little Mouse. "Please forgive me this one time. I won't ever forget it. And, who knows, someday I may be able to do a favor for you?"

"You, help me?" The Lion roared with laughter. "You're so small. What could you ever do to help me?"

"You never know," said the Mouse. "You never know."

The great Lion was so amused at the thought of a little Mouse helping him that he lifted up his paw and let the Mouse go free.

Some time later the Lion was walking through the jungle when a huge net fell on him. He was caught in a trap. Hunters tied him to a tree while they went to look for a wagon to carry the Lion on.

The little Mouse happened to pass by. He saw the Lion tied to the tree, and he wanted to help.

"Chew the ropes," pleaded the Lion. "And hurry."

The Mouse began to gnaw at the ropes that held the great King of Beasts. Just as the hunters were returning, the Lion broke free. He gave a great roar, and the hunters ran away, seeing that the Lion was no longer tied up.

"You were right," said the Lion. "Even the small can help the big. I'm glad I let you go."

"So am I," said the Mouse, and they each went their separate ways into the jungle. ❖

Notes on Telling:

This story is good for beginning tellers because it's short and easy to remember. You can develop a squeaky mouse voice and a large, deep lion voice. Keeping the two straight may be easier if you also assume a slightly different posture for each animal, perhaps upright and bold for the lion, and hunched and looking up for the mouse. You can add gestures for the mouse scurrying, the lion trapping the mouse, the lion tied up, and the mouse chewing the ropes. SS

The Boy Who Cried "Wolf!"

Here's another Aesop story, which I also heard from my father. You can find versions of the story in many folktale collections. There's a clear lesson in the story that children can grasp easily, without an explicit moral. SS

There was once a shepherd boy who watched the village sheep in the fields up in the hills. He got bored and wanted some excitement. He started to shout, "Wolf! Wolf! The Wolf is chasing the sheep!"

The villagers came running up the hill to help the boy drive the wolf away. When they got there, there was no wolf. They were very angry that they had run all the way up the hill for nothing. The boy laughed at them.

"Don't cry 'wolf', when there's no wolf," said the villagers. They went grumbling back down the hill.

The shepherd boy quickly grew bored again. He shouted out, "Wolf! Wolf! The wolf is chasing the sheep!"

He laughed as he watched the villagers run up the hill to help him drive the wolf away.

When the villagers saw that there was no wolf they said, "Don't cry 'wolf' when there is NO wolf!"

But the boy just laughed and watched them go down the hill again.

A short time later, a real wolf appeared, circling the edge of the field.

The shepherd boy jumped to his feet and shouted as loud as he could, "Wolf! Wolf!"

But the villagers thought he was trying to fool them again, and they didn't come.

That evening, the villagers wondered why the shepherd boy hadn't come back to the village with the sheep. They climbed up the hill to find the boy, who was crying.

"There really was a wolf here! The flock ran away! I shouted, 'Wolf!' but no one came. Why didn't you come and help me?"

An old man put his arm around the young shepherd.

"We'll help you look for the lost sheep in the morning," he said. " But nobody believes a liar...even when he's telling the truth!"

The boy promised to himself that he wouldn't cry "Wolf" again, unless, of course, he really saw a wolf. ❖

Notes on Telling:

The repetition in this story can allow children to help with calling "wolf," laughing, and making cross faces of the villagers. Children probably need to know something about being a shepherd to understand the story. I have mixed feelings about the wolf as the enemy, as wolves have gotten a bad rap in folktales for a long time. Nevertheless the story carries on a long and strong tradition that I wouldn't want to alter. SS

Why Koala Has No Tail

It's fascinating to realize that there are as many as 900 Aboriginal groups in Australia. This Aboriginal legend, like many folktales, explains why something in the natural world is the way it is. The French call these "pourquoi" stories, meaning "why." It is enormous fun to play with this idea of creating explanations for things in our world, and it's a great way to fuel your own imagination as a creator of stories. FS

There was a time when the rain did not fall. For days and days and weeks and weeks, no rain fell at all. Everything grew dry, even the river and streambeds where the waters usually flowed.

Koala and Tree Kangaroo were thirsty – Oh, so thirsty! They went to all of their usual places, but there was no water anywhere to be found. But then Tree Kangaroo remembered that when he was small, his mother had taken him to a place. He told Koala about that place, where he and his mother had dug for water in a dry time like this. "And we found just enough water for a sip for my mother and a sip for me," Tree Kangaroo said.

Koala got very excited. "Do you think you could find that place again?" he said. Tree Kangaroo nodded, and Koala said, "Let's go!"

So they began to walk and walk and walk. They came to a dry streambed, and Koala asked,

"Is this the place? Is this the place?
I'd love to stop here for a drink."
"It's not the place," said Tree Kangaroo,
"a little bit farther, I think."

So they walked and walked and walked some more. Again they came to a dry streambed, and once again Koala asked,

"Is this the place? Is this the place?
I'd love to stop here for a drink."
"It's not the place," said Tree Kangaroo,
"a little bit farther, I think."

So they walked and walked and walked some more. Oh, this was such a long way to walk! They came to another dry stream bed, and Koala, once again, asked,

"Is this the place? Is this the place?
I'd love to stop here for a drink."
"This is the place," said Tree Kangaroo,
and gave the Koala a wink.

Koala sat down and said, "That was such a long, long, walk. And I am very tired. Why don't you dig first, Tree Kangaroo?"

So the Tree Kangaroo started to dig:

So he dug and he dug, and he threw out the rocks,

It was hot but he dug some more.

He dug 'til he thought he could use some help.

He asked, but Koala just snored.

Koala was asleep in the shade, with his long tail covering his eyes. "I'll let him rest a little longer," said Tree Kangaroo, and he started to dig again.

So he dug and he dug, and he threw out the rocks,

It was hot but he dug some more.

He dug 'til he thought he could use some help.

He asked, but Koala just snored.

Finally, Koala woke up and he walked over to the place where Tree Kangaroo had been digging. But after he had taken just a few steps, he cried out, "Oooooo! I've got a thorn in my tail! I just can't dig right now. You go ahead." So, that's what Tree Kangaroo did.

So he dug and he dug, and he threw out the rocks,

It was hot but he dug some more.

He dug 'til he thought he could use some help.

He asked, just like he had before.

"I've taken three turns, Koala," said Tree Kangaroo. "It's your turn now."

"I'm coming," said Koala. "I want to dig! Ooohhh!! I just got a cramp in my tail! You'd better do a little more digging. I'll help out as soon as this cramp goes away." So, that's what Tree Kangaroo did.

So he dug and he dug, and he threw out the rocks,

It was hot but he dug some more.

He dug 'til he thought he could use some help.

He asked, just like he had before.

"Koala, you come over here and do some of this digging," said Tree Kangaroo. "I've had four turns now. It's your turn!"

Koala came over and looked down into the deep hole that Tree Kangaroo had dug. He said, "You know, you've done all that work, and now the hole is so nice and deep. Surely you're about to find water. You really should be the one to find the water. Just go ahead and finish up." And Koala sat down. And Tree Kangaroo? Well...

He dug and he dug, and he threw out the rocks,

It was hot but he dug some more.

He dug 'til he thought he could use some help.

He dug, just like he had before.

Then, all of a sudden, water began to seep into Tree Kangaroo's hole.

"I did it, I did it!" shouted Tree Kangaroo! "Oh, Koala, there is almost enough for one sip already, and soon I'm sure there will be enough for both of us to have a drink!"

Well, Koala hopped up, ran over to that hole, shoved Tree Kangaroo out of the way, and began to drink up that water. There he was, head down in the hole, with his tail sticking straight up.

Tree Kangaroo got angry – really angry. He reached over to Koala's tail, and snatched it, pulling it right off.

"Oowwwww!" Koala yelped. And he came right up out of that hole. He looked over at Tree Kangaroo, who was holding Koala's tail tightly in his fist. Tree Kangaroo glared at Koala. Koala didn't say a word. He knew he had been selfish. He knew he had been lazy. He knew he had not been kind to his friend.

Well, you know Koala's tail never did grow back. And that's why, even today, Koalas don't have tails. That reminds them to be kind to their friends.❖

Notes on Telling:

With just two characters, this story is a good one for creating specific voices for koala and tree kangaroo. Spend some time deciding how you want each one to sound, and getting it "firm," so that you don't, at any point in the telling, speak without using the character voice of the animal. I have found children are immediately enthralled by the addition of a silly voice. It's like I am announcing that we are going to play together, and this is going to be FUN! FS

How Rabbit Lost His Tail

This story is an American folk tale with roots in African-American and Native American tradition. There's a similar story about how Bear lost his tail in the ice. SS

A long time ago, Rabbit had short ears and a long tail.

One day, Rabbit was very hungry. He met Fox, who was carrying a long string of fish.

"How did you get all those nice fish, Mr. Fox?" said Rabbit.

"Come with me, I'll show you," replied Fox.

Fox led Rabbit to a pond, which was frozen over. He cut a hole in the ice. "Now, you sit here all night and drop your long tail as deep as you can in the water. In the morning you'll have a nice string of fish hanging on it."

Rabbit sat all night on the pond, with his tail hanging down into the cold water. When he felt a tug, he assumed it must be fish biting his tail.

But in the morning, Rabbit was stuck. The ice had frozen around his tail, holding him fast. He pulled and pulled but couldn't get loose.

"Help, help," called Rabbit.

Owl heard him and came. Owl pulled Rabbit's ears, but he couldn't get Rabbit out. All he could do was make Rabbit's ears longer by stretching them out, which is why Rabbit's ears are long to this day.

Other animal friends came: first Beaver, then Raccoon, Deer, and finally Squirrel. They all pulled and pulled. Finally, with a "Pop" Rabbit came loose.

Unfortunately, his tail remained in the ice. And that's why Rabbits have long ears, and short tails, to this very day.

Not only that, but you'll never see a Rabbit eating fish anymore. ❖

Notes on Telling:

It may be useful to show children pictures of the animals involved in the story. Children in the South may have a hard time imagining a lake freezing over, but it definitely happens up North. Again, a picture may help children imagine the scene. Tellers can use different voices for Rabbit and Fox. High and low, or fast and slow tones can illustrate the difference between the characters. Add facial expressions and motions for sitting and waiting on the ice, and especially for pulling Rabbit loose. SS

Katchi Katchi Blue Jay

This tale is based on a tale of the Nisqually Indian tribe of the Pacific Northwestern United States. There are many folktales from all over the globe that tell of light, the solstice, or the balance of day and night. They represent the "wonderings" of peoples through time about the mysteries of the natural world. FS

When the world was new the moon came up every night, making light for the animals. The animals were very pleased with this, as it allowed them to hunt for food and go about their business.

But one night, the moon did not come up. The animals waited, but the moon did not come up! It was so dark, they could not see. They could not hunt, or go about the business of their lives.

The chief called all of the animals together, and said, "The moon must have overslept tonight, for she has not come up. It is too dark for us. Someone must go and wake the moon."

It must be someone fast – we need help quickly!

It must be someone strong – it is a very long way to Moon's house.

It must be someone smart, for the Moon has a clapping door.

You know, that door will clap shut and catch anyone who tries to enter.

Well, when the chief spoke about fast, and strong, and smart, the Blue jay jumped right up. "That's me, that's me!

"I am Blue Jay, the fastest, smartest, strongest bird,

Off now to the moon, I don't have time to hear a word,

No one can tell me anything that I don't know,

I'm fast and smart and strong – Don't stop me now,

I gotta go!"

"Well, alright, Blue Jay," said the Chief. "But I need to give you a bit of advice first, about Moon's clapping door. Come sit with me, so I can explain." You see, the chief knew that whoever went to see the moon would need to take something to prop open that clapping door, or it would slap shut when you tried to enter!

"I am Blue Jay, the fastest, smartest, strongest bird,

Off now to the moon, I don't have time to hear a word,

No one can tell me anything that I don't know,

I'm fast and smart and strong – Don't stop me now,

I gotta go!"

I don't need any help to get through that door!" And off Blue Jay flew.

Blue Jay had a great idea. He flew to the top of the tallest tree, and from the top of that tree, he flew to the next tallest tree up the mountain, climbing higher and higher each time.

When Blue Jay got to the top of the tallest tree on the tallest mountain, he bumped into something – something soft and feathery and something that called out, "Whoooooooo?"

It was, of course, the owl that lived at the top of the tallest tree on the tallest mountain. Blue Jay immediately launched into his story: "The moon – he didn't wake up tonight, and it's dark, and no one can see anything and I'm going to take care of things!"

"Oh," said owl, "Come sit by me and let me tell you about Moon's clapping door."

"Oh, no!" said Blue Jay,

"I am Blue Jay, the fastest, smartest, strongest bird,

Off now to the moon, I don't have time to hear a word,

No one can tell me anything that I don't know,

I'm fast and smart and strong – Don't stop me now,

I gotta go!"

I don't need any help to get through that door!" And off Blue Jay flew.

Blue Jay could see Moon's house now, so he took his biggest, strongest, flying leap, and landed right in front of Moon's house. But Moon's house did have a clapping door, and it opened, and CLAPPED shut, opened, and CLAPPED shut, opened and CLAPPED shut…

Blue Jay watched and counted along with the rhythm of that door. He tried to get it just right, and he JUMPED!!

And WHACK! That door clapped shut right on Blue Jay's head! Oh, NO!

Katchi, Katchi, Katchi!!!

Blue Jay hopped around holding onto his poor, squished head! His feathers were all squished straight up into a funny shape, straight up in the air!! Ohhhhh, it hurt!

Katchi, Katchi, Katchi!

Blue Jay was holding onto his poor head, stumbling around with his eyes squeezed shut, calling,

Katchi, Katchi, Katchi!

And suddenly, he stumbled right through that door, and Moon woke up with all of his squawking, sat up and said, "What are you DOING here?"

Katchi, Katchi, Katchi!

You must be the moon! I was sent to wake you up! We're all stumbling around in the dark, because you overslept, and now your door has squished my head!

Katchi, Katchi, Katchi!

"Hold on a minute, Blue Jay! Didn't your chief tell you about how to get through my door?" said Moon.

"I didn't have time to listen to all that! I had to hurry to get here!"

"Ah...... But the owl," said Moon, "you must have passed him on your way here. Didn't he tell you about how to get through my door?

"I told you I was in a hurry, " said Blue Jay. "I didn't have time to listen to owl or anyone else!"

"Well, Friend Jay," said Moon, "I do believe you need to learn to listen to others sometimes. It will make things go much better for you. From now on, you will wear that silly looking puff of feathers on your head, to remind you and others that it is a good plan to listen to the advice of your elders."

"Katchi, Katchi, Katchi!" said Blue Jay. This is all your fault. If you hadn't overslept, we wouldn't have been in the dark, and I wouldn't have had to come wake you!

"Oh, Blue Jay!" said Moon, "That is no way to talk to your elders. Don't you know that it is important to speak respectfully to your elders?"

"From now on, you will wear your puff of feathers, and you will say just one thing, 'Katchi, Katchi, Katchi! And when anyone hears your Katchi, Katchi, Katchi! It will remind them to always speak respectfully to elders!"

"Katchi, Katchi, Katchi!" said Blue Jay, for that was all he could say.

"I sleep late one night every month, Blue Jay, so don't come here waking me again. It is the dark of the moon, my night to sleep in." Moon helped Blue Jay out through the door, and Blue Jay flew back home, calling "Katchi, Katchi, Katchi!"

And you know, even to this day, if you see a Blue Jay, he's still wearing that funny puff of feathers sticking straight up on his head, and still calling out, in a loud, disrespectful voice, "Katchi, Katchi, Katchi!" That's to remind us that it is a good thing to listen respectfully to our elders. ❖

Notes for Telling:

Try creating a chant or song sung in a voice you create for Blue Jay. How can that voice, and the gestures you use while singing or chanting, reflect the impatient Blue Jay's personality?   I've found that the term "Katchi, Katchi" can become a shared code word in the classroom or family for remembering to be a good listener, a far more palatable reminder than a traditional admonishment! FS

Why the Sky Is Far Away

This tale from Nigeria holds an acknowledgement of the challenge of our careless forgetfulness as humans. It also beautifully reminds us to use our resources wisely. My favorite learning from this story is the importance of gratitude. FS

A long, long time ago, the sky was very low to the ground. So low, in fact, that people could reach right up and touch it. And even better, people could reach up and break off a piece of the sky – and they could eat it - wonderful, delicious, yummy pieces of sky.

Sky, yummy sky, eat as I walk by

There is sky as far as anyone can see

Sky, yummy sky, eat as I stroll by.

There is plenty more for you and you and me

And that's just what the people did, too. They never had to work to feed themselves. Life was simple and sweet.

For a very long time, things went very well for the people and the sky. The sky was happy to offer the food the people needed, and the people were grateful for the delicious food the sky provided, and they took just what they needed to be healthy and strong.

Sky, yummy sky, eat as I walk by
There is sky as far as anyone can see
Sky, yummy sky, eat as I stroll by.
There is plenty more for you and you and me.

But time passed, and the people started breaking off bigger and bigger pieces of the sky. They would eat what they wanted, and throw the rest on the ground, where it would just rot, and go to waste. They figured it didn't really matter, since it seemed there was plenty of sky.

Sky, yummy sky, eat as I walk by
There is sky as far as anyone can see
Sky, yummy sky, eat as I stroll by.
There is plenty more for you and you and me.

The sky, however, did not appreciate the wastefulness of the people. She did not like to see the pieces of herself on the ground rotting, where the people had thrown them down and left them. She thought the rotting sky made the earth look ugly, too. The sky was sure the people would figure this out, but time passed, and it only seemed to get worse. So finally, the sky told the people, "Hey you! People! All of you! Listen to me! I am tired of watching you waste pieces of me! I am tired of watching pieces of me rot on the ground, and make the earth look bad! I am asking you to take only what you need, and no more. Do you understand? This is important! If you keep doing this, I will NOT keep feeding you!

The people were terrified! "OK, Sky," they said. "We

understand! And we won't do it anymore – we promise!" And for a long time they did. They didn't waste any sky, took only what they needed, and didn't leave any pieces of the sky on the ground to rot.

But time passed, and the people slowly began to get careless again, forgetting their promise to the Sky. They would think Sky wouldn't notice if they took a little more than they needed. Or they would try to hide the extra left on the ground, hoping Sky wouldn't see it.

Sky, yummy sky, eat as I walk by
There is sky as far as anyone can see
Sky, yummy sky, eat as I stroll by.
There is plenty more for you and you and me.

But Sky did see, and one day, when she saw a person break off a great big piece, more than he could possibly eat, and then throw that leftover down to rot, she got mad – really mad.

Sky turned dark, and rumbled and churned and lightening bolts came down and winds blew. And as she rumbled and roared, the people noticed something else – that she was rising!! The people reached up, but could not touch Sky, as she went higher and higher and higher. They tried everything, climbing up into trees and standing on top of their houses, but none of them could reach any part of Sky.

There the people were, looking up at the sky that was so far away. They realized that they had nothing to eat. They were afraid, and as the day wore on, they grew hungrier and hungrier.

The sky did take pity on the humans though, and at the end of that day, she began to rain down seeds, and then she rained water to help the seeds grow, and provided sunlight for the seeds, too. And she told the people, "I have given you what you need. You have seeds to grow plants for food, water for the plants to drink, and sunlight to help them grow tall and strong. But you must care for the plants, and work in the fields to grow the food that you need. Don't ever forget to take care of the gifts you have been given."

And so it is that even today, people have to work for the food that they eat.

Sky, yummy sky, eat as I walk by
There is sky as far as anyone can see
Sky, yummy sky, eat as I stroll by.
There is plenty more for you and you and me. ❖

Notes for Telling:

This story offers opportunities for children to inject their own visions of some of the action. For example, when the sky "rumbles and churns," you might step out of the telling for a moment and ask your listeners, "How do you think the sky looked when it rumbled and churned? Can you show me with your bodies, right there in your spot where you're sitting, how the sky might have looked as it rumbled and churned?"

When you invite children to demonstrate their ideas in this way, it's useful to have an agreed upon start and stop cue, such as "Go!" and "Freeze!" And it is important that you clarify, before the invitation to move is offered, the physical space that a child may use for their demonstration. FS

Just Enough

This much-loved Jewish Tale has many versions. As is congruent with my storytelling style, you'll find a participatory chant or song provided here. How does this type of telling work for you? Perhaps you'll like this idea, and find yourself injecting such chants or songs in some of your other chosen stories, too. FS

Long ago there lived a tailor named Joseph. He worked every day making clothes – coats, dresses and fine clothes for his well-off neighbors, but he never seemed to have enough money to make himself a good warm coat.

Well, finally Joseph had saved enough money for the cloth for his very own coat. He went to the market and bought the fabric – beautiful, warm wool that was a dark, rich shade of brown. He took the cloth home, and at the end of his workdays, he would stay late in his shop to work on his new coat.

When the coat was finally finished, Joseph stood in front of the mirror admiring his work. Oh, it was a lovely coat! From that day on, Joseph wore the coat everywhere.

Every day he wore that coat
Through sun and snow and rain
Until that coat was all worn out
and only rags remained.

Joseph looked sadly at his dear old coat. It had holes in the elbows, and the hem was all frayed and ragged-looking. Joseph thought about the coat, and then he had an idea. Joseph took the old, worn-out coat back to his workbench, and went to work. He cut and cut, and stitched and stitched, and as he worked, he sang:

Still enough to make a vest
If I just snip and sew
There's just enough to make it work
By using what I know.

When the vest was finally finished, Joseph stood in front of the mirror admiring his work. Oh, it was a lovely vest! From that day on, Joseph wore the vest everywhere.

Every day he wore that vest
Through sun and snow and rain
Until that vest was all worn out
and only rags remained.

Joseph looked sadly at his dear old vest. It had holes across the back, and the hem was all frayed and ragged looking. Joseph thought about the coat, and then he had an idea. Joseph took the old, worn-out vest back to his workbench, and went to work. He cut and cut, and stitched and stitched, and as he worked, he sang:

Still enough to make a cap
If I just snip and sew
There's just enough to make it work
By using what I know.

When the cap was finally finished, Joseph stood in front of the mirror admiring his work. Oh, it was a lovely cap! From that day on, Joseph wore the cap everywhere.

Every day he wore that cap
Through sun and snow and rain
Until that cap was all worn out
and only rags remained.

Joseph looked sadly at his dear old cap. It had holes on top, and the band was all frayed and ragged looking. Joseph thought about the cap, and then he had an idea. Joseph took the old, worn-out cap back to his workbench, and went to work. He cut and cut, and stitched and stitched, and as he worked, he sang:

Still enough to make a tie
If I just snip and sew
There's just enough to make it work
By using what I know.

When the tie was finally finished, Joseph stood in front of the mirror admiring his work. Oh, it was a lovely tie! From that day on, Joseph wore the tie everywhere.

Every day he wore that tie
Through sun and snow and rain
Until that tie was all worn out
and only rags remained.

Joseph looked sadly at his dear old tie. It had threads hanging from the bottom, and soup stains where Joseph had spilled his dinner. Joseph thought about the tie, and then he had an idea. Joseph took the old, worn-out tie back to his workbench, and went to work. He cut and cut, and stitched and stitched, and as he worked, he sang:

Still enough to make a button
If I just snip and sew
There's just enough to make it work
By using what I know.

When the button was finally finished, Joseph put it on his coat with that wonderful button, and stood in front of the mirror, admiring his work. Oh, it was a lovely button! From that day on, Joseph wore the button everywhere.

Every day he wore that button
Through sun and snow and rain
Until that button was all worn out
and only rags remained.

Joseph looked sadly at his dear old button. It was frayed and ragged. Joseph thought about his button. "Old button," he said, "you have been my coat, and then my vest, my cap and then my tie, and finally a fine button. There is nothing left to save." But then Joseph had an idea.

Still enough to make a story
If I just make it so,
There's just enough to make it work
By using what I know.

"I will carry you and tell everyone about the things I have made with my cloth. And I can show them the button when I tell them my story. You see, there is always just enough for a story!" ❖

Notes for Telling:

Try extending this telling by having children contribute the words for their most beloved garments. Young children often have an item of clothing that they treasure, so this is a fun way to enliven the story. Using their own stated articles of clothing, insert them in the chant, and create an accompanying gesture to describe the garment. Young children will love this personalized creation, and the sharing of it with their classmates. FS

RESOURCES

Our online storytelling course can be accessed by going to either Stuart's or Faye's websites:

www.stuartstotts.com

www.fayestanley.com

There are many publishers worthy of note in the storytelling world, most prominently August House Publishers at **http://www. augusthouse.com**. You will find resources categorized on their website by function and culture. You will also find useful learning links, including lesson plans incorporating stories. Finally, there are books that specifically support your development as a storyteller, and/or your work with student storytellers.

Yellow Moon Press is another publisher that publishes stories, books and recordings, exclusively. You'll find them at **http://www.yellowmoon.com**.

Books

Birch, Carol, L., *The Whole Story Handbook: Using Imagery to Complete the Story Experience*, August House Publishers, 2000.

Caduto, Michael J. and Bruchac, Joseph, *Keepers of the Earth: Native American Stories and Environmental Activities for Children*, Fulcrum, Inc., 1998.

DeSpain, Pleasant, *Eleven Nature Tales: A Multicultural Journey*, August House Publishers, Inc., 1996.

DeSpain, Pleasant, *Thirty-Three Multicultural Tales to Tell*, August House Publishers, Inc., 1993.

DeSpain, Pleasant, *Twenty-Two Splendid Tales to Tell from Around the World*, August House Publishers, Inc., 1994.

Eades, Jennifer M. Fox, *Classroom Tales: Using Storytelling to Build Emotional, Social and Academic Skills across the Primary Curriculum*, Jessica Kingsley Publishers, 2006.

Gordh, Bill, *15 Easy Folktale Fingerplays with Cross-Curricular Activities*, Scholastic Professional Books, 1997.

Gordh, Bill, *Stories in Action: Interactive Tales and Learning Activities to Promote Early Literacy*, Libraries Unlimited, 2006.

Hamilton, Martha, & Weiss, Mitch, *Children Tell Stories: Teaching and Using Storytelling in the Classroom*, Richard C. Owen Publishers, 2nd edition, 2005.

Heinig, Ruth Beall, *Improvisation with Favorite Tales: Integrating Drama into the Reading/Writing Classroom*, Heinemann, 1992.

Holt, David, and Mooney, Bill, *Ready-To-Tell Tales: Sure-Fire Stories From America's Favorite Storytellers*, August House Publishers, Inc., 1994.

Laminack, Lester L., *Unwrapping the Read Aloud*, Scholastic, 2009.

Livo, Norma, *Joining In: An Anthology of Audience Participation Stories and How to Tell Them*, Yellow Moon Press, 5th printing, 1993.

MacDonald, Margaret Read, *Look Back and See: Twenty Lively Tales for Gentle Tellers*, The H. W. Wilson Company, 1991.

MacDonald, Margaret Read, *Shake-It-Up Tales!: Stories to Sing, Dance, Drum, and Act Out*, August House Publishers, Inc., 2000.

MacDonald, Margaret Read, *The Storyteller's Start-Up Book: Finding, Learning, Performing and Using Folktales*, August House Publishers, 1993.

MacDonald, Margaret Read, Whitman, Jennifer MacDonald, & Whitman, Nathaniel Forrest, *Teaching with Story: Classroom Connections to Storytelling*, August House Publishers, 2013.

MacDonald, Margaret Read, *Three Minute Tales: Stories from Around the World to Tell or Read When Time Is Short*, August House Publishers, 2004.

Miemi, Loren, and Ellis, Elizabeth, *Inviting the Wolf In: Thinking About Difficult Stories*, August House Publishers, 2001.

Milford, Susan, *Tales Alive: Ten Multicultural Folktales with Activities*, Williamson Publishing, 1995.

Milford, Susan, *Tales of the Shimmering Sky: Ten Global Folktales with Activities*, Williamson Publishing, 1996.

Miller, Violet Teresa deBarba, *Holiday Stories All Year Round: Audience Participation Stories and More*, Libraries Unlimited, 2008.

Mooney, Bill and Holt, David, *The Storyteller's Guide: Storytellers Share Advice for The Classroom, Boardroom, Showroom, Podium, Pulpit, and Center Stage*, August House Publishers, 1996.

Norfolk, Bobby and Sherry, *The Moral of the Story: Folktales for Character Development*, August House Publishers, 1999.

Pearman, Elisa Davy, *Once Upon a Time: Storytelling to Teach Character and Prevent Bullying*, Character Development Group, Inc., 2006.

Rubright, Lynn, *Beyond the Beanstalk: Interdisciplinary Learning Through Storytelling*, Heinemann, 1996.

Saldaña, Johnny, *Drama of Color: Improvisation with Multiethnic Folklore*, Heinemann, 1995.

Websites

These websites have video links to stories being told by professional tellers. In addition, updated web links can be found at:

www.FayeStanley.com/storytelling-resources/

www.StuartStotts.com/storytelling-resources/

Online Resources

Storytelling Workshop with Gerald Fierst
http://teacher.scholastic.com/writewit/storyteller/meet.htm

Storyteller.net **http://www.storyteller.net/**

Story Arts Online **http://www.storyarts.org/**

Handbook for Storytellers
http://falcon.jmu.edu/~ramseyil/storyhandbook.htm

**http://www.pbs.org/circleofstories/educators/
lesson1.html#top**

http://www.mcli.dist.maricopa.edu/smc/journey/

Online Video Resources

Bill Harley TED talk on Storytelling
http://www.youtube.com/watch?v=B6NCF391SX0

http://www.billharley.com/Videos.asp?VideoID=4

Teaching Storytelling in the Classroom
http://www.youtube.com/watch?v=JrZc6eztoH4

Grimm Story **http://www.storyteller.net/news/2012/03/696/**

About the Authors

Faye Stanley is an educator, singer, storyteller and community music leader, author, and teaching artist. She presents conference keynotes and facilitates workshops, coaches and trains teachers and teaching artists, and works with state and national organizations to design and evaluate arts integrated learning initiatives. She currently designs and leads professional development on arts integration for organizations including the Kennedy Center and others, and has conducted and published research on creative process and culturally responsive learning in New Zealand, Hawaii, and with Native Americans and African Americans in the US. Faye holds an undergraduate degree in Music Therapy and Music Education, a Masters in Education, and an interdisciplinary PhD in Education, the Arts, and Cultural Studies. Find out more about her at **http://www.fayestanley.com**.

Stuart Stotts is an author, songwriter, storyteller, and teaching artist. His songs have been recorded by artists around the world, and his recordings have won national awards. He's been working in schools for nearly 30 years. Stuart frequently presents at early childhood conferences and trainings on topics ranging from literacy to music to arts integration to storytelling. He's a Kennedy Center teaching artist and the author of seven books, including "We Shall Overcome: A Song that Changed the World," which was an ALA Notable Book in 2011. Find out more at **www.StuartStotts.com**.

Jill Kramer, illustrator, received her MA in Art Education from the School of the Art Institute of Chicago and a BFA in printmaking from Kent State University. She has been teaching for over 15 years in museum & community art settings. In 2009, she was chosen by the National Park Service to act as artist in residence at Acadia National Park in Maine. Jill works from her home studio in Oak Park, Illinois where she lives with her husband and two children. Her work can be viewed at **www.jillakramer.com**.

Made in the USA
Las Vegas, NV
02 December 2023

81955855R00044